# Bob's Spiritfly

Written by
Laura Kristi Cronin

Illustrated by
Dominic Glover

**PUBLISHING**

First Edition
August 2017
Sleek Publishing
www.BobsSpiritfly.com

Laura Kristi Cronin
Dominic Glover
Bob's Spiritfly
Written by  Laura Kristi Cronin
Illustrations & Design by Dominic Glover.
1st Ed.
p. cm.
Ages 3 & Up

Summary: This book tackles the very sensitive subject of losing a pet
with poetic grace and inspiring illustrations!

ISBN 978-0-9990479-0-3
Printed by IngramSpark 2017

# "To the pet you'll never forget!"

In loving memory of our sweet dog, Bella.

A tribute to my gramps, Eugene Carara.

Dedicated to Kaiya Love and Enzo Eugene.

My deepest gratitude goes to the talented Dominic Glover, who brought my words to life, as well as to my editor, Ronald A. Busse, for his grammatical expertise and professional guidance. A very heartfelt thanks to my twinny, Ileah, for sharing her divine 808 connection with me so many years ago. To my husband, mom and dad, and to the many beautiful souls who kindly offered advice, gave insight, and invested energy into this little book with a big message.

I am forever grateful!

Bob's Spiritfly has been published in *Bumples* online magazine, issue #44, Summer 2017.

Life as a pup
Was so happy and fun.
I lived a long life,
But those dog days are done.


So I decided to pay a visit
To my family, but not as me.
I will go as a butterfly
Believing in magic is the key.

# Flap, Flap, Flitter...

I zoom through a window that's open.
It's Anna's room and there she is,
Looking sad and mopin'.

She's looking at my picture,
It makes my tiny heart throb
When I hear her say aloud,
"You were my favorite dog, Bob."

Now it's 8:08,

My time is finally here!

I've been waiting for this chance

To wipe away her tears!


I turn her frown upside down,

I perch upon her nose!

Her eyes go cross, her face lights up,

Her smile I just unfroze!

Joy returns,

We dance and play!

Life's good again,

What a wonderful day!

Eugene sees me and squeals,
How I love to see his joy!
He picks me up and grins,
Oh, how I love that boy!

The clock strikes 8:08,
Time to put on my show!
Those numbers are very important,
Just thought you ought to know.

Flap, Flap, Flitter...

I turn, zip, and dive

# He holds out his hand
# for a butterfly high five!

Our time is so special
That I don't want to leave,
But I'll come back tomorrow
And show these kids how to believe!

Early the next morning
I find them fishing at the pond.
Today is the day I'll tell them
about my very special bond!

Eugene wants to catch "the big one"
But his watch is in the way,
So he puts it on a tree stump
Then he backs away...

He throws a perfect cast,
But there is no time to wait!
His watch displays the time,
It's exactly 8:08!

# Flap, Flap, Flitter...

It's time for them to see

That I am Bob,

And that Bob is me!

I circle the family,
I look in their eyes,

I perch on the watch to present my big suprise...

With everyone watching
I crawl up the screen,
Settle into place
And lock eyes with Eugene.

I spread my wings wide,
Displaying the numbers proudly.

Eugene looks up and says,
"I've got it!" very loudly.
"The numbers spell Bob's name!
8:08 means B-O-B!"
They look at one another,
Wondering... could it be?

With that I took flight,
Making eights in the sky,
Trying to show them
That I AM Bob's Spiritfly!

How cool is this,
That they've figured it out!
Bob's spirit lives on,
There's no need to pout!

They all laughed and played
Until the sun began to set,
And everyone agreed
To live life with no regret.

I taught them that passings
Don't have to be so tragic,

And that all you have to do
Is believe in a touch of magic!

CPSIA information can be obtained
at www.ICGtesting.com
Printed in the USA
LVXC01n1224191017
552962LV00001B/2